McGraw-Hill's EASY FRENCH STORYBOOK

Goldilocks and the Three Bears

Boucle d'Or et les trois ours

THE FUN WAY TO LEARN 50 NEW FRENCH WORDS!

Ana Lomba

Illustrated by Santiago Cornejo • French Translation by Dominique Wenzel • Audio Produced by Rob Zollman

McGraw·Hill

New York   Chicago   San Francisco   Lisbon   London   Madrid   Mexico City
Milan   New Delhi   San Juan   Seoul   Singapore   Sydney   Toronto

4 5 6 7 8 9 0   CTP/CTP   10

ISBN 0-07-146173-6 (book and CD)
ISBN 0-07-146174-4 (book alone)
Library of Congress Control Number: 2005927554

Interior design by General Learning Communications

A mon mari, John Mulcahy,

parce que tu crois en mes rêves et que tu t'y associes.

Affectueusement.

To my husband, John Mulcahy,

because you believe in my dreams and join in them.

With love.

Introduction

Welcome to the world of **easy and fun** French for young children!

Young children learn languages best when they are active participants—just as they learned their native language. Children learning a second language in a classroom or structured setting do not have the same opportunities to hear and use the language as they have for their native language. Parents can offer important supplemental exposure by providing high-quality language instruction at home. The target language introduced needs to be age appropriate and engaging so children can use it (and will want to use it) in different situations.

McGraw-Hill's Easy French Storybooks are designed to smoothly immerse children in French by using simple narration and everyday dialogues to relate familiar stories, accompanied by illustrations that help tell the story. By creating a direct link between the story lines and the illustrations, children can infer meaning from both text and images, leading to greater understanding. Moreover, the use of common, everyday language exchanges in the stories eases children's language acquisition. *McGraw-Hill's Easy French Storybooks* contain the proper amount of conversational language for a beginning level of instruction.

Start by referring to the mini-picture dictionary at the end of the book. Point to the illustrations as you listen to the vocabulary words on the companion CD. After listening a few times, test the children's comprehension by asking them to point to the illustrations as you say the words. Change the order of the words to ensure comprehension.

Ask simple questions like *Qui est-ce?* (Who is it?) or *Qu'est-ce que c'est?* (What is it?) to elicit verbal responses. If your children don't respond, offer the answer. Children need time to figure out the links between the new words and concepts, as well as to register and practice new sounds. So encourage, but don't force speaking. Praise goes a long way; make sure to use lots of compliments: *Très bien!* (Very good!)

It is not necessary to know all the vocabulary in the mini-picture dictionary to start listening to the story. You can first listen to the English version of the story if that will help you become familiar with the story. Once you start reading the French story, I recommend sticking to French. Do not switch back and forth between languages. If you do this, your children may not make the effort to understand and learn French.

Listen to the French story several times. After you're familiar with it, start reading the story in French to your children. Don't let pronunciation stop you. You will become more proficient with practice. Your children will have a big advantage over you in pronunciation, as they are able to hear and register sounds that you cannot distinguish—consider this a "blind spot" in your hearing because you were not exposed to those sounds earlier in life. Use a lot of expression and animation. Your children will love to see you speaking French! If your children can read on their own, you may want to let them read the book themselves.

The story in this book is very theatrical. In my classes, teachers become actors: they impersonate the protagonists of the story and transform the classroom into a stage. In one-on-one situations you can jazz up the story by using puppets or acting out the story yourself. I have observed in my classes that children become more talkative when they are using puppets or masks. This gives them more freedom, as they can act as somebody else! The use of puppets or masks is an excellent strategy for shy children. Create a make-believe corner in your home with puppets, masks, and costumes related to the story. This allows children to explore the new language hands-on in spontaneous play.

To further expand learning, use *McGraw-Hill's Easy French Storybooks* in combination with *Play and Learn French* (available from McGraw-Hill). *Play and Learn French*, also based on our "easy immersion" methodology, contains conversations, games, and songs that you can use with your children every day. You can also enjoy *McGraw-Hill's Easy French Storybook: Little Red Riding Hood / Le Petit Chaperon Rouge*.

Enjoy discovering new worlds together!

Il était une fois une petite maison dans une forêt.

Once upon a time there was a little house in a forest.

Dans la maison vivaient trois ours bruns. Papa Ours était grand, Maman Ourse était moyenne et Petit Ours était tout petit.

In the house lived three brown bears. Papa Bear was big, Mama Bear was medium-sized, and Little Bear was small.

Un jour Maman Ourse prépara de la soupe et la servit dans une grande assiette creuse, une moyenne et une petite. *"À table! La soupe est prête!"*

One day, Mama Bear prepared soup and served it in a big bowl, a medium-sized bowl, and a small bowl. "Time to eat! The soup is ready!"

3

**Papa Ours goûta la soupe dans la grande assiette creuse
et il dit, "Aïe, aïe, aïe, je me suis brûlé, je me suis
brûlé! Cette soupe est très chaude!"**

Papa Bear tasted the soup in the big bowl and he said, "Ouch,
ouch, ouch, I burned myself, I burned myself! This soup is very hot!"

"Si on allait faire un tour pendant qu'elle refroidit," dit Maman Ourse. Et les ours partirent faire un tour dans la forêt.

"Let's go for a walk while it cools down," said Mama Bear. So the bears went for a walk in the forest.

5

Dans une autre petite maison en bordure de la forêt vivait Boucle d'Or.

In another little house outside the forest lived Goldilocks.

Un jour Boucle d'Or partit se promener dans la forêt. Soudain elle sentit quelque chose. *"Que ça sent bon! J'ai très faim!"*

One day Goldilocks went for a walk in the forest. Suddenly she smelled something. "It smells so good! I am very hungry!"

Boucle d'Or entra dans la petite maison et elle vit la soupe sur la table. ***"De la soupe! Chic alors, j'adore la soupe!"***

Goldilocks went into the house and saw the soup on the table. "Soup! Great, I love soup!"

Boucle d'Or goûta la soupe dans la grande assiette et elle dit, *"Aïe, je me suis brûlée! Cette soupe est trop chaude!"*

Goldilocks tried the soup in the big bowl and said, "Ouch, I burned myself! This soup is too hot!"

Puis elle goûta la soupe dans la moyenne assiette et elle dit, *"Pouah, cette soupe est trop froide!"*

Then she tried the soup in the medium-sized bowl and said, "Yuck, this soup is too cold!"

Enfin elle goûta la soupe dans la petite assiette et elle dit, *"Mmm, cette soupe est délicieuse!"* Et Boucle d'Or mangea toute la soupe. *"Il n'y en a plus!"*

Finally, she tried the soup in the little bowl and she said, "Mmm, this soup is delicious!" And Goldilocks ate all the soup. "All done!"

"Je suis très fatiguée," dit Boucle d'Or. Alors Boucle d'Or vit une grande chaise, une moyenne chaise et une petite chaise. **"Je vais m'asseoir."**

"I am very tired," said Goldilocks. Goldilocks then saw a big chair, a medium-sized chair, and a small chair. "I'm going to sit down."

Boucle d'Or s'assit sur la grande chaise.
"Aïe, cette chaise est trop dure!"

Goldilocks sat on the big chair. "Ouch, this chair is too hard!"

Puis elle s'assit sur la moyenne chaise.
"Cette chaise est trop molle!"

Then she sat on the medium-sized chair. "This chair is too soft!"

Enfin elle s'assit sur la petite chaise. *"Cette chaise est parfaite. Elle n'est pas dure et elle n'est pas molle."*

Finally, she sat on the small chair. "This chair is just right. It is not too hard and it is not too soft."

Et Boucle d'Or commença à se balancer sur la chaise.
"En avant, en arrière,

And Goldilocks started to rock in the chair. "Forth and back,

en avant, en arrière, en avant…"

forth, back, forth . . ."

"Aïe!" La chaise se cassa et Boucle d'Or tomba.
"Qu'est-ce que je vais faire!"

"Ouch!" The chair broke and Goldilocks fell down.
"What am I going to do!"

"*Ahhh!*" dit Boucle d'Or en bâillant.
"*Que j'ai sommeil!*"
Boucle d'Or alla dans la chambre et elle
vit un grand lit, un moyen lit et un petit lit.
"*Je vais me coucher.*"

"Ahhh!" yawned Goldilocks. "I am so sleepy!"
Goldilocks went to the bedroom and she saw a big bed,
a medium-sized bed, and a small bed. "I'm going to lie down."

Boucle d'Or s'allongea d'abord sur le grand lit.
"Aïe, ce lit est trop dur!"

Goldilocks lay on the big bed first. "Ouch, this bed is too hard!"

Ensuite elle s'allongea sur le moyen lit.
"Ce lit est trop mou!"

Then she lay on the medium-sized bed. "This bed is too soft!"

Enfin elle s'allongea sur le petit lit. **_"Chic alors!
Ce lit est parfait!"_** Et elle s'endormit.

Finally, she lay down on the small bed. "This is great!
This bed is perfect!" And she fell asleep.

À ce moment-là, les trois ours arrivèrent à la maison.
"Que ça sent bon! J'ai très faim!" dit Petit Ours.

Then the three bears arrived at the house.
"It smells so good! I am very hungry!" said Little Bear.

Les ours se mirent à table. *"Grrr, quelqu'un a goûté ma soupe, et il y a un cheveu dedans!"* grogna Papa Ours très en colère.

The bears sat down to eat. "Grrr, somebody has tasted my soup, and there's a hair in it!" grunted Papa Bear, very angry.

"Grrruuu, quelqu'un a goûté ma soupe, et il y a un cheveu dedans!" grogna Maman Ourse effrayée.

"Grrrrrrr, somebody has tried my soup, and there's a hair in it!" grunted Mama Bear, very scared.

"*Grrr houhouhou, quelqu'un a mangé ma soupe! Il reste seulement un cheveu dedans!*" grogna Petit Ours en pleurant.

"Grrr boo hoo hoo, somebody ate my soup! There's only a hair inside!" grunted Little Bear, crying.

"Grrr, il se passe quelque chose de bizarre!"
grogna Papa Ours pensif.

"Grrr, something strange is happening!" grunted Papa Bear,
pensive.

"Je suis très fatiguée. Allons nous asseoir," dit Maman Ourse.

"I am very tired. Let's sit down," said Mama Bear.

"Grrr, quelqu'un s'est assis sur ma chaise et il y a un cheveu dessus!" grogna Papa Ours très en colère.

"Grrr, somebody has been sitting on my chair, and there's a hair on it!" grunted Papa Bear, very angry.

"Grrrrruuu, quelqu'un s'est assis sur ma chaise et il y a un cheveu dessus!" grogna Maman Ourse effrayée.

"Grrrrrrr, somebody has been sitting on my chair, and there's a hair on it!" grunted Mama Bear, very scared.

"Grrr houhouhou, quelqu'un s'est assis sur ma chaise et l'a cassée! Bouhouhou!" grogna Petit Ours en pleurant.

"Grrr boo hoo hoo, somebody has been sitting on my chair and has broken it! Boo hoo hoo!" grunted Little Bear, crying.

**"Grrr, il se passe quelque chose de bizarre!"
grogna Papa Ours pensif.**

"Grrr, something strange is happening!" grunted Papa Bear,
pensive.

Alors les trois ours entrèrent dans la chambre. *"Grrr, quelqu'un s'est allongé sur mon lit et il y a un cheveu dessus!"* grogna Papa Ours très en colère.

Then the three bears went into the bedroom. "Grrrr, somebody has been lying on my bed, and there's a hair on it!" grunted Papa Bear, very angry.

"Grrrrruuu, quelqu'un s'est allongé sur mon lit et il y a un cheveu dessus!" grogna Maman Ourse effrayée.

"Grrrrrrrr, somebody has been lying on my bed, and there's a hair on it!" grunted Mama Bear, very scared.

"Grrr houhouhouhouhou, quelqu'un s'est allongé sur mon lit, et elle y est encore! Bouhouhou!" grogna Petit Ours en pleurant.

"Grrrr boo hoo hoo hoo hoo, somebody has been lying on my bed, and she is still there! Boo hoo hoo!" grunted Little Bear, crying.

Boucle d'Or se réveilla en entendant tout ce vacarme.
"Trois ours, ahhh!" **cria-t-elle terrorisée.**

Goldilocks woke up to the commotion. "Ahhh, three bears!"
she screamed in terror.

Boucle d'Or sauta par la fenêtre. **"Au secours!**
À l'aide! Trois ours!"

Goldilocks jumped out the window. "Help! Help! Three bears!"

Et elle courut et courut et ne revint plus jamais.

And she ran and ran and never came back.

"Eh bien!" dirent les trois ours surpris.
"Cette fille court vraiment très vite!"
Et voilà, cette histoire est finie.

"Wow!" said the three surprised bears. "That girl runs very fast!" The End.

la maison

house

la forêt

forest

trois ours

three bears

la soupe

soup

l'assiette creuse

bowl

Boucle d'Or

Goldilocks

la chaise

chair

le lit

bed

les cheveux

hair

la fenêtre

window

la cuiller

spoon

la louche

ladle

About the Author

Award-winning, language-learning innovator
Ana Lomba is the founder and director of
Sueños de Colores LLC, a company offering
language-learning instruction and resources for
parents and teachers of young children. She is
the coauthor of the books *Play and Learn
Spanish* and *Play and Learn French*, published
by McGraw-Hill, 2005 Parents' Choice
Approved award winners. Ana is an advocate
for early foreign language education and holds
leadership positions in prominent U.S. regional
and national language associations, including
the American Council on the Teaching of
Foreign Languages (ACTFL), the National
Network for Early Language Learning (NNELL),
and Foreign Language Educators of New Jersey
(FLENJ). Ana holds advanced degrees in
Spanish and Latin American literature from
Binghamton University and Princeton University.
A native of Madrid, Spain, Ana currently lives
with her husband and three children in
Princeton, New Jersey.